JUL   1999

THE ADVENTURES OF
MR TOAD

FROM THE WIND IN THE WILLOWS

It was perhaps the most conceited song that any animal ever composed.

THE ADVENTURES OF
MR TOAD

FROM THE WIND IN THE WILLOWS

BY

KENNETH GRAHAME

ILLUSTRATED BY

INGA MOORE

CANDLEWICK PRESS
CAMBRIDGE, MASSACHUSETTS

This book comprises the second half
of Kenneth Grahame's classic work for children,
The Wind in the Willows, first published in 1908.
It has been carefully abridged by the illustrator,
who has ensured that the words almost always
remain those of the author.

Illustrations copyright © 1998 by Inga Moore

First U.S. edition 1998

Library of Congress Cataloging-in-Publication Data
Grahame, Kenneth, 1859—1932.
The adventures of Mr Toad from the wind in the willows / Kenneth Grahame;
abridged and illustrated by Inga Moore—1st U.S. ed.
p. cm.
Summary: Follows the escapades of Mr Toad as he escapes from
jail, is reunited with Mole, Ratty, and Badger, and together with
them battles the weasels to reclaim Toad Hall. Companion to "The River Bank."
ISBN 0-7636-0581-6
[1. Animals—Fiction.] I. Grahame, Kenneth, 1859-1932. Wind in the willows. II. Title.
PZ7.M7846Ad 1998   [Fic]—dc21   98-23599

·   2 4 6 8 10 9 7 5 3

Printed in Hong Kong

This book was typeset in M Bembo.
The pictures were done in ink and pastel crayon.

Candlewick Press
2067 Massachusetts Avenue
Cambridge, Massachusetts 02140

Contents

ONE

Mr Toad

It was a bright morning in the early part of summer; the river had resumed its wonted banks, and a hot sun seemed to be pulling everything green and bushy up out of the earth, as if by strings. The Mole and the Water Rat had been up since dawn, busy on matters connected with boats and the boating season; painting and varnishing, mending paddles, repairing cushions, hunting for missing boat-hooks, and so on; and were finishing breakfast in their little parlour and discussing their plans for the day, when a heavy knock sounded at the door.

"Bother!" said the Rat, all over egg. "See who it is, Mole, like a good chap, since you've finished."

The Mole went to attend the summons, and the Rat heard him utter a cry of surprise. Then he flung the parlour door open, and announced with much importance, "Mr Badger!"

This was a wonderful thing, indeed, that the Badger should call on them, or on anybody. He generally had to be caught, if you wanted him, as he slipped quietly along a hedgerow of an early morning or a late evening, or else hunted up in his own house in the middle of the wood.

The Badger strode into the room, and stood looking at the two animals with an expression full of seriousness.

"The hour has come!" he said.

"What hour?" asked the Rat uneasily, glancing at the clock.

"*Whose* hour, you should say," replied the Badger. "Why, Toad's hour! The hour to take Toad in hand!"

"Hooray!" cried the Mole delightedly. "*We'll* teach him to be a sensible Toad!"

"This very morning," continued the Badger, "another new and exceptionally powerful motor-car will arrive at Toad Hall on approval or return."

"We ought to do something," said the Rat gravely. "He had another smash-up only last week, and a bad one. That coach-house of his is piled to the roof with fragments of motor-cars, none of them bigger than your hat!"

"He's been in hospital three times," put in the Mole; "and as for the fines he's had to pay, it's simply awful to think of."

"Yes," continued the Rat, "Toad's rich, we all know; but he's not a millionaire. And he's a hopelessly bad driver, and quite regardless of law and order. Killed or ruined—it's got to be one of the two, sooner or later."

"We must be up and doing," said the Badger, "ere it is too late. You two will accompany me instantly to Toad Hall."

"Right you are!" cried the Rat, starting up. "We'll rescue the poor animal!"

"We'll take him seriously in hand," went on the Badger. "We'll stand no nonsense whatever. We'll bring him back to reason, by force if need be. We'll *make* him be a sensible Toad."

They set off up the road on their mission, and reached Toad Hall to find, as the Badger had anticipated, a shiny new motor-car, of great size, painted a bright red, standing in front of the house. As they neared the door, it was flung open, and Mr Toad, arrayed in goggles, cap, gaiters, and enormous overcoat, came swaggering down the steps.

"Hullo! you fellows!" he cried. "You're just in time to come for a jolly—a jolly—for a—er jolly—"

The Badger strode up the steps. "Take him inside," he said to his companions. Then he turned to the chauffeur in charge of the new motor-car.

"I'm afraid you won't be wanted today," he said. "Mr Toad has changed his mind. He will not require the car."

"Now, then!" he said to the Toad, when the four of them stood in the hall, "first, take those ridiculous things off!"

"Shan't!" replied Toad, with spirit. "What is the meaning of this? I demand an explanation."

They had to lay Toad out on the floor, kicking and calling all sorts of names, before they could get his motor-clothes off him bit by bit, and they stood him up on his legs again. Now he was merely Toad, and no longer the Terror of the Highway, he giggled feebly.

"You knew it must come to this sooner or later, Toad," the Badger explained severely. "You've disregarded all the warnings we've given you, you're getting us animals a bad name in the district by your furious driving and your smashes and your rows with the police. But we never allow our friends to make fools of themselves beyond a certain limit; and that limit you've reached. You've often asked us to come and stay with you, Toad; well, now we're going to. When you are sorry for what you've done, and see the folly of it, and you promise never to touch a motor-car again, we may quit, but not before. Take him upstairs, you two, and lock him in his bedroom."

"It's for your own good, Toady," said the Rat kindly, as Toad, kicking and struggling, was hauled upstairs by his two friends. "Think what fun we shall all have together, just as we used to, when you've quite got over this—this painful attack of yours! No more of those incidents with the police," he said, as they thrust him into his bedroom.

"No more weeks in hospital, being ordered about by nurses," added the Mole, turning the key on him.

They descended the stair, Toad shouting abuse at them through the keyhole.

"It's going to be a tedious business," said the Badger, sighing. "I've never seen Toad so determined. However, we will see it out. He must never be left an instant unguarded. We shall take it in turns to be with him, till the poison is out of his system."

They arranged watches accordingly. Each animal took it in turns to sleep in Toad's room at night, and they divided the day between them. At first Toad was very trying to his guardians. He would arrange bedroom chairs in rude resemblance of a motor-car and crouch on them, bent forward, staring fixedly ahead, making uncouth, ghastly noises, till the climax was reached, when, turning a complete somersault, he would lie prostrate amidst the ruins of the chairs, completely satisfied for the moment. As time passed, however, these seizures grew less frequent, and his friends strove to divert his mind into fresh channels. But his interest in other matters did not seem to revive, and he grew apparently languid and depressed.

One fine morning the Rat, whose turn it was to go on duty, went upstairs to relieve Badger, whom he found fidgeting to be off and stretch his legs. "Toad's still in bed," he told the Rat, outside the door. "Can't get much out of him, except, 'O, leave him alone.' Now, you look out, Rat! When Toad's quiet, he's at his artfullest."

"How are you today, old chap?" inquired the Rat cheerfully, as he approached Toad's bedside.

A feeble voice replied, "Thank you, Ratty! So good of you to inquire! How are you yourself, and the excellent Mole?"

"O, *we're* all right," replied the Rat. "Mole is going out for a run with Badger. So you and I will spend a pleasant morning together. Now jump up, there's a good fellow!"

"Dear Rat," murmured Toad, "I am far from 'jumping up.' I beg you—step round to the village and fetch the doctor."

"What do you want a doctor for?" inquired the Rat, coming closer and examining him. He certainly lay very still and flat, and his voice was weaker and his manner changed.

"Surely you have noticed—" murmured Toad. "Tomorrow, indeed, you may be saying, 'O, if only I had noticed sooner! If only I had done something!' But never mind—forget I asked."

"Look here, old man," said the Rat, beginning to get rather alarmed, "of course I'll fetch a doctor, if you really want him."

"And—would you mind," said Toad, with a sad smile, "at the same time asking the lawyer to step up? There are moments—a moment—when one must face disagreeable tasks."

"A lawyer! He must be bad!" the Rat said to himself, as he hurried from the room, not forgetting to lock the door behind him. "I've known Toad fancy himself frightfully bad before; but I've never heard him ask for a lawyer! If there's nothing really the matter, the doctor will tell him and cheer him up. I'd better go; it won't take long." So he ran off to the village on his errand of mercy.

The Toad, who had hopped lightly out of bed as soon as he heard the key turned in the lock, watched him from the window till he disappeared down the carriage-drive. Then he dressed quickly in his smartest suit, filled his pockets with cash from a drawer, and next, knotting the sheets from his bed together and tying one end round the central mullion of the Tudor window which formed such a feature of his bedroom, he scrambled out, slid to the ground, and, taking the opposite direction to the Rat, marched off whistling a merry tune.

It was a gloomy luncheon for Rat when the Badger and the Mole returned. The Badger's remarks may be imagined; even the Mole could not help saying, "You've been a bit of a duffer this time, Ratty! Toad, too, of all animals!"

"He did it awfully well," said the crestfallen Rat.

"He did *you* awfully well!" rejoined the Badger hotly.

Meanwhile, Toad, gay and irresponsible, was walking along the high road, some miles from home. At first he had taken by-paths, and crossed many fields, and changed his course several times, in case of pursuit; but now, feeling safe from recapture, and the sun smiling brightly on him, and all nature joining in a chorus of approval to the song of self-praise, his own heart was singing; he almost danced along the road in his satisfaction and conceit.

"Smart piece of work that!" he remarked to himself, chuckling. "Poor old Ratty! My! won't he catch it when the Badger gets back! A worthy fellow, Ratty, but very little intelligence and no education. I must take him in hand someday, and see if I can make something of him."

Full of conceited thoughts such as these, he strode along, his head in the air, till he reached a little town . . .

where the sign of "The Red Lion," swinging across the main street,

reminded him that he had not breakfasted that day.

He marched into the inn, ordered the best luncheon that could be provided, and sat down to eat it in the coffee-room.

He was about half-way through his meal when an only too familiar sound, approaching down the street, made him start trembling all over. The "poop-poop!" drew nearer, and the car could be heard to turn into the inn-yard and stop. Presently the party entered the coffee-room, talkative and gay, voluble on their experiences of the morning. Toad listened, all ears; at last he could stand it no longer. He slipped out of the room, paid his bill at the bar, and sauntered round to the inn-yard. "There cannot be any harm," he said to himself, "in my only just *looking* at it!"

The car stood in the middle of the yard, quite unattended. Toad walked slowly round it.

"I wonder," he said to himself presently, "I wonder if this sort of car *starts* easily?"

Next moment, hardly knowing how it came about, he found he had hold of the handle and was turning it. As the familiar sound broke forth, the old passion seized Toad and he found himself, somehow, seated in the driver's seat; as if in a dream, he pulled the lever and swung the car round the yard and out through the archway. He increased his pace, and as the car devoured the street and leapt forth on the high road through the open country, he was Toad once more, Toad at his best, Toad the terror, the traffic-queller, the Lord of the lone trail, before whom all must give way.

The miles were eaten up as he sped he knew not whither,

living his hour, reckless of what might come to him.

"To my mind," observed the Chairman of the Bench of Magistrates, "the *only* difficulty in this case is how we can make it sufficiently hot for the rogue and hardened ruffian we see cowering in the dock before us.

"He has been found guilty of stealing a valuable motor-car; of driving to the public danger; and of gross impertinence to the rural police. Mr Clerk, tell us, please, what is the stiffest penalty we can impose for each of these offences?"

The Clerk scratched his nose with his pen. "Twelve months for the theft, three years for the furious driving and fifteen years for the cheek – those figures tot up to nineteen years – so you had better make it a round twenty and be on the safe side," he concluded.

"Excellent!" said the Chairman. "Prisoner! It's going to be twenty years for you this time. And mind, if you appear before us again, upon any charge whatever, we shall have to deal with you very seriously!"

The Toad was dragged from the Court House to the grim old castle, whose ancient towers soared high overhead. There in the heart of the innermost keep, the rusty key creaked in the lock, the great door clanged behind him; and Toad was a helpless prisoner in the remotest, best-guarded dungeon in all the length and breadth of Merry England.

TWO

Toad's Adventures

When Toad found himself in a dungeon, and knew that all the grim darkness of a medieval fortress lay between him and the world of sunshine and high roads where he had lately been so happy, he flung himself at full length on the floor, and shed bitter tears. "This is the end of everything," he said, "at least it is the end of Toad, which is the same thing. O unhappy and forsaken Toad!" He passed his days and nights for several weeks, refusing his meals or intermediate light refreshments, though the jailer, knowing Toad's pockets were well lined, frequently pointed out that many comforts, indeed luxuries, could be sent in—at a price—from the outside.

27

Now the jailer had a daughter. This kind-hearted girl said to her father one day, "I can't bear to see that poor beast so unhappy and getting so thin! You let me have the managing of him. I'll make him eat."

Her father replied that she could do what she liked with him. He was tired of Toad and his sulks. So she went and knocked on the door of Toad's cell.

"Cheer up, Toad," she said, entering. "Sit up and try a bit of dinner. See, I've brought you some of mine, hot from the oven!" It was bubble-and-squeak, between two plates, and its fragrance filled the narrow cell. The penetrating smell of cabbage reached the nose of Toad as he lay prostrate in his misery on the floor, and gave him the idea for a moment that life was not such a desperate thing as he had imagined. But still he wailed, and kicked his legs, and refused to be comforted. So the wise girl retired, but, of course, the smell of hot cabbage remained, as it will do, and Toad, between sobs, sniffed and reflected and gradually began to think new thoughts; of chivalry and poetry, and deeds still to be done; of meadows, and cattle browsing in them; kitchen-gardens, and straight herb-borders, and warm snap-dragon beset by bees. The air of the cell took on a rosy tinge: he began to think of his friends, and how they would surely be able to do something; of lawyers, and what a fool he had been not to get a few; and lastly, he thought of his own cleverness and resource, and all that he was capable of if he only gave his great mind to it; and the cure was almost complete.

When the girl returned, some hours later, she carried a tray, with a cup of tea steaming on it; and a plate piled up with hot buttered toast. The smell of that toast simply talked to Toad; talked of warm kitchens; breakfast on bright frosty mornings, cosy firesides on winter evenings, when one's ramble was over and slippered feet were propped on the fender. Toad sat up, dried his eyes, sipped his tea and munched his toast, and soon began talking freely about himself, and the house he lived in, his doings there, and what a lot his friends thought of him.

The jailer's daughter encouraged him to go on.

"Tell me about Toad Hall," she said. "It sounds beautiful. But first wait till I fetch you some more tea and toast."

She tripped away, and returned with a fresh trayful; and Toad, pitching in, told her about the boathouse, the fish-pond and the old walled kitchen-garden; about the pig-sties and the stables, the pigeon-house, and the hen-house; and about the dairy and the wash-house, the china cupboards, and the linen-presses (she liked that bit especially); about the banqueting hall, and the fun they had there when the other animals were gathered round the table and Toad was at his best, singing songs, telling stories, carrying on generally. Then she wanted to know about his friends, and was very interested in all he had to tell her about them and how they were, and what they did to pass their time. When she said good night, having filled his water-jug and shaken up his straw for him, Toad curled himself up and had an excellent night's rest and the pleasantest of dreams.

29

They had many interesting talks together as the dreary days went on; and the jailer's daughter grew very sorry for Toad, and thought it a shame that a poor animal should be locked up in prison for what seemed to her a trivial offence.

One morning she said, "Toad, listen. I have an aunt who is a washerwoman."

"Never mind," said Toad affably. "*I* have several aunts who *ought* to be washerwomen."

"Do be quiet, Toad," said the girl. "As I said, I have an aunt; she does the washing for the prisoners in this castle. Now, she's very poor. A few pounds would mean a lot to her. If you could come to some arrangement by which she would let you have her dress and bonnet, you could escape from the castle as the official washerwoman. You're very alike in many respects— particularly about the figure."

"We're *not,*" said Toad. "I have a very elegant figure— for what I am." "So has my aunt," replied the girl, "for what *she* is. But have it your own way. You horrid, proud, ungrateful animal, when I'm sorry for you, and trying to help you!"

"Yes, yes, thank you very much indeed," said Toad. "But look here! you wouldn't surely have Toad, of Toad Hall, going about the country disguised as a washerwoman!"

"Then you can stop here as Toad," replied the girl.

Toad was always ready to admit himself in the wrong. "You are a good, kind, clever girl," he said, "and I am a stupid toad. Introduce me to your worthy aunt, if you will be so kind."

Next evening the girl ushered her aunt into Toad's cell, bearing his week's washing pinned up in a towel. The sight of certain gold sovereigns thoughtfully placed on the table left little to discuss. In return for his cash, Toad received a cotton print gown, an apron, a shawl and a rusty black bonnet; the only stipulation the old lady made being that she should be gagged and bound and dumped in a corner.

"Now, Toad," said the girl. "Take off that coat and waistcoat of yours; you're fat enough as it is."

Shaking with laughter, she proceeded to "hook-and-eye" him into the gown, arranged the shawl with a professional fold, and tied the bonnet
under his chin.

"You're the very image of her," she giggled, "only I'm sure you never looked so respectable in all your life. Now, good-bye, Toad, and good luck. Go straight down the way you came up; and if anyone says anything to you, as they probably will, being men, you can chaff back a bit, of course, but remember you're a widow woman, with a character to lose."

31

With a quaking heart, Toad set forth on what seemed to be a hare-brained and hazardous undertaking; but he was soon surprised to find how easy everything was made for him. The washerwoman's squat figure in its familiar cotton print seemed a passport for every barred door and grim gateway; even when he hesitated, uncertain as to the right turning to take, he found himself helped by the warder at the next gate, anxious to be off to his tea, summoning him to come along sharp and not keep him waiting all night.

At last he heard
the wicket-gate in the
great outer door click behind
him, felt the air of the outer world
upon his brow, and knew that he was free!

33

Dizzy with the easy success of his daring exploit, he walked quickly towards the town. As he walked along, his attention was caught by some red and green lights a little way off, and the sound of puffing and snorting of engines fell on his ear. "Aha!" he thought, "this is a piece of luck! A railway-station."

He made his way to the station, consulted a time-table, and found that a train, bound more or less in the direction of home, was due to start in half an hour. "More luck!" said Toad, and went off to the booking-office to buy his ticket.

He gave the name of the station nearest Toad Hall, and put his fingers where his waistcoat pocket should have been and found—not only no money, but no pocket to hold it, and no waistcoat to hold the pocket!

To his horror he recollected that he had left both coat and waistcoat behind him in his cell, and with them his money, keys, matches, watch, pencil-case—all that makes life worth living. He made one desperate effort to carry the thing off, and, in his fine old manner he said, "Look here! I find I've left my purse behind. Just give me that ticket, will you, and I'll send the money on tomorrow. I'm well known in these parts."

The clerk stared at him and the rusty black bonnet. "I should think you were well known," he said, "if you've tried this game often. Stand away from the window, madam; you're obstructing the other passengers!"

Baffled and full of despair, he wandered down the platform where the train was standing and tears trickled down his nose.

"Hullo, mother!" said the engine-driver, "what's the trouble?

You don't look particularly cheerful!"

"O, sir!" said Toad, "I am a poor unhappy washerwoman, and I've lost all my money, and can't pay for a ticket, and I *must* get home tonight somehow, and whatever I am to do I don't know. O dear, o dear!"

"That's a bad business," said the engine-driver. "Lost your money—and can't get home—and got some kids, too, waiting for you, I dare say?"

"Any amount," sobbed Toad. "And they'll be hungry—and playing with matches—and upsetting lamps—and quarrelling. O dear, O dear!"

"I'll tell you what," said the good engine-driver. "You're a washerwoman. And I'm an engine-driver and there's no denying it's terribly dirty work. If you'll wash a few shirts for me when you get home, and send 'em along, I'll give you a ride on my engine. It's against the Company's regulations, but we're not so particular in these out-of-the-way parts."

Toad scrambled up into the cab of the engine. Of course, he had never washed a shirt in his life, and couldn't if he tried; but he thought: "When I get home to Toad Hall, and have money again, and pockets to put it in, I will send the engine-driver enough to pay for quite a quantity of washing, and that will be the same thing, or better."

The guard waved his welcome flag, the engine-driver whistled in cheerful response, and the train moved out of the station. As the speed increased, and Toad could see fields, and hedges, and cows, and horses, all flying past him, and as he thought how every minute was bringing him nearer to Toad Hall and friends, and money to chink in his pocket, and a soft bed to sleep in, and good things to eat, and praise and admiration of his adventures and his cleverness, he began to skip up and down and sing snatches of song, to the great astonishment of the engine-driver, who had come across washerwomen before, but never one like this.

They had covered many a mile, and Toad was considering what he would have for supper, when he noticed the engine-driver, with a puzzled expression on his face, was leaning over the side of the engine, listening hard. "It's strange," he said, "we're the last train running tonight, yet I could be sworn I heard another following us."

A dull pain in the lower part of Toad's spine made him want to sit down and try not to think of all the possibilities.

By this time the moon was shining brightly, and presently the engine-driver called out, "I can see it now! It's an engine. It looks as if we're being pursued."

The miserable Toad, crouching in the coal-dust, tried hard to think of something to do, with dismal want of success.

"They are gaining on us fast!" cried the engine-driver. "And the engine is crowded with the queerest lot of people! Warders and policemen all waving and shouting the same thing—

"Stop, stop, stop!"

Toad fell on his knees and cried, "Save me, save me, Mr Engine-driver, I am not the washerwoman I seem to be! I am a toad; and I have just escaped from a loathsome dungeon; and if those fellows on that engine recapture me, it will be chains and bread-and-water misery once more."

The engine-driver looked down on him very sternly, and said, "Now tell the truth; what were you put in prison for?"

"It was nothing much," said Toad, colouring deeply. "I only borrowed a motor-car. I didn't mean to steal it, really."

The engine-driver looked very grave and said, "By rights I ought to give you up. But I don't hold with motor-cars, and I don't hold with being ordered about on my own engine. So cheer up, Toad! I'll do my best, and we may beat them yet!"

They piled on more coals, shovelling furiously; the furnace roared, the sparks flew, the engine leapt and swung, but still their pursuers gained. The engine-driver wiped his brow and said, "It's no good, Toad. They are running light and have the better engine. There's just one thing left to do, it's your only chance, so be ready to jump when I tell you."

The train shot into a tunnel, and the engine roared and rattled, till they shot out at the other end. The driver shut off steam and braked, and as the train slowed down he called, "Now, jump!"

Toad jumped, rolled down a short embankment, picked himself up unhurt, scrambled into a wood and hid.

Peeping out, he saw his train get up speed and disappear at a great pace. Then out of the tunnel burst the pursuing engine, roaring and whistling, her motley crew waving and shouting, "Stop! stop! stop!" When they were past, Toad had a hearty laugh—for the first time since he was thrown into prison.

But he soon stopped when he came to consider that it was now very late and dark and cold, and he was in an unknown wood, with no money and no supper, and still far from friends and home; and the dead silence of everything, after the roar and rattle of the train, was something of a shock.

An owl, swooping towards him, brushed his shoulder with its wing, making him jump. Once he met a fox, who stopped, looked him up and down in a sarcastic sort of way, and said, "Hullo, washerwoman! Half a pair of socks and a pillow-case short this week! Mind it doesn't occur again!" and swaggered off, sniggering. At last he sought the shelter of a hollow tree, where he made himself as comfortable a bed as he could and slept soundly till morning.

─ THREE ─

The Further Adventures of Toad

The door of the hollow tree faced eastwards, so Toad was called at an early hour. Sitting up, he rubbed his eyes, looking round for familiar stone wall and barred window; then, with a leap of the heart, remembered everything—his escape, his flight, his pursuit; best of all, that he was free!

Free! He marched forth into the morning sun. He had the world to himself, that early summer morning. The dewy woodland was solitary and still; the green fields were his own to do as he liked with; the road, when he reached it, in that loneliness that was everywhere, seemed to be looking for company. Toad, however, was looking for something that could tell him clearly which way he ought to go.

The road was presently joined by a little canal. Round a bend in the canal came plodding a solitary horse, stooping forward as if in anxious thought. From his collar stretched a long line, taut, but dipping with his stride, the further part of it dripping pearly drops. Toad let the horse pass, and stood waiting for what the fates were sending him.

With a swirl of water, the barge slid up alongside of him, its occupant a big stout woman wearing a linen sun-bonnet.

"A nice morning, ma'am!" she remarked to Toad.

"I dare say it *is*, ma'am!" responded Toad, "to them that's not in trouble, like what I am. My married daughter, she sends for me to come at once; so off I comes, fearing the worst, as you will understand, ma'am, if you're a mother too. And I've left my washing business to look after itself, and my young children, ma'am; and I've lost all my money, and my way."

"Where might your married daughter be living, ma'am?" asked the barge-woman.

"Near Toad Hall, ma'am," replied Toad.

"Toad Hall? I'm going that way," replied the barge-woman. "Come along in the barge with me, and I'll give you a lift."

She steered the barge close to the bank, and Toad stepped lightly on board.

"So you're in the washing business?" said the barge-woman. "And are you *very* fond of washing?"

"I love it," said Toad. "I simply dote on it. Never so happy as when I've got both arms in the wash-tub."

"What a bit of luck," observed the barge-woman.

"Why, what do you mean?" asked Toad nervously.

"Well, there's a heap of things of mine that you'll find in a corner of the cabin. If you'll just put them through the wash-tub as we go along, it'll be a real help to me."

"I might not do 'em as you like," said Toad. "I'm more used to gentlemen's things myself. It's my special line."

"You do the washing you are so fond of," replied the barge-woman. "Don't deprive me of the pleasure of giving you a treat!"

Toad was fairly cornered. He looked for escape, saw he was too far from the bank for a flying leap, and resigned himself to his fate. "If it comes to that," he thought in desperation, "I suppose any fool can *wash!*"

He fetched tub, soap, and other necessaries from the cabin, selected a few garments, and set to.

A half-hour passed, and every minute of it saw Toad getting crosser and crosser. Nothing he could do to the things seemed to do them good. He tried coaxing, slapping, punching. His back ached and he noticed with dismay that his paws were beginning to get all crinkly. Now Toad was very proud of his paws. He muttered under his breath words that should never pass the lips of washerwomen or Toads; and lost the soap, for the fiftieth time.

The barge-woman laughed till tears ran down her cheeks.

"Pretty washerwoman you are!" she gasped. "Never washed so much as a dish-clout in your life, I'll lay!"

Toad's temper, which had been simmering for some time, now boiled over.

"You common, low, *fat* barge-woman!" he shouted; "don't you dare to talk to your betters like that! Washerwoman indeed! I would have you know that I am a Toad, a very well-known, respected, distinguished Toad! I may be under a bit of a cloud at present, but I will *not* be laughed at by a barge-woman!"

The woman peered under his bonnet. "Why, so you are!" she cried. "Well, I never! a horrid, nasty, crawly Toad! And in my nice clean barge, too! That is a thing that I will *not* have."

One big mottled arm shot out and caught Toad by a fore-leg. Then the world turned upside down, the barge seemed to flit across the sky, and Toad found himself flying through the air.

The water, when he reached it, proved cold, though not enough to quell his spirit. He rose to the surface, and when he had wiped the duckweed out of his eyes the first thing he saw was the barge-woman looking back at him over the stern of the barge and laughing.

He struck out for the shore, touched land, and climbed up the steep bank. Then, gathering his wet skirts well over his arms, he started to run after the barge, as fast as his legs would carry him, wild for revenge.

The barge-woman was still laughing when he drew up level with her. "Put yourself through your mangle, washerwoman," she called out, "and iron your face and crimp it, and you'll pass for quite a decent-looking Toad!"

Toad never paused to reply. Revenge was what he wanted, not cheap, windy, verbal triumphs, though he had a thing or two he would have liked to say. Running swiftly on he overtook the horse, unfastened the tow-rope, jumped on the horse's back, and urged it to a gallop by kicking it vigorously in the sides. He steered for the open country, abandoning the tow-path, and swinging his steed down a rutty lane. "Stop, stop, stop!" shouted the barge-woman.

"I've heard that song before," said Toad, laughing,

as he continued to spur his steed onward.

The barge-horse was not capable of any sustained effort, and its gallop soon subsided into a trot, and its trot to an easy walk; but Toad was quite contented with this. He had recovered his temper, now he had done something he thought really clever; and he was satisfied to jog along quietly in the sun, trying to forget how very long it was since he had had a square meal.

He had travelled some miles, his horse and he, and he was feeling drowsy in the hot sunshine, when the horse stopped, lowered his head, and began to nibble the grass; and Toad just saved himself from falling off.

He looked about him and found he was on a wide common,
dotted with patches of gorse and bramble as far as he could see.
Near him stood a dingy gypsy caravan, and a man was sitting,
very busy smoking and staring into the wide world.
A fire of sticks was burning near by, and over the fire
hung an iron pot, and out of that pot came forth
smells—warm, rich, and varied smells.
Toad sniffed, and looked at
the gypsy; and the
gypsy smoked,
and looked
at him.

Presently the gypsy remarked in a careless way, "Want to sell that there horse of yours?"

It had not occurred to Toad to turn the horse into cash.

"O no," he said, "I'm too fond of him, and he dotes on me. All the same, how much might you be disposed to offer me?"

The gypsy looked the horse over, and he looked Toad over with equal care. "Shillin' a leg," he said briefly.

"A shilling a leg?" cried Toad. "I must work that out."

He climbed down off his horse and did sums on his fingers. At last he said, "That comes to four shillings. O no; I could not think of accepting four shillings for this young horse of mine."

"Well," said the gypsy, "I'll make it five shillings, and that's three-and-sixpence more than the animal's worth."

Toad pondered. He was hungry and penniless, and still some way from home, and enemies might be looking for him. To one in such a situation, five shillings may very well appear a large sum of money. On the other hand, it did not seem very much to get for a horse. But then, the horse hadn't cost him anything. At last he said firmly, "You hand me six shillings and sixpence, and as much breakfast as I can eat out of that iron pot of yours. In return, I will make over to you my spirited young horse, with all the harness and trappings on him, freely thrown in. If that's not good enough, say so, and I'll be getting on. I know a man near here who's wanted this horse for years."

The gypsy grumbled frightfully, and declared he'd be ruined. But in the end he lugged a dirty canvas bag out of the depths of his trouser-pocket, and counted out six shillings and sixpence into Toad's paw. Then he disappeared into the caravan, and returned with a large iron plate. He tilted the pot, and a stream of hot rich stew gurgled into it. Toad took the plate on his lap, and stuffed, and stuffed, and stuffed, and kept asking for more, and the gypsy never grudged it him. He thought he had never eaten so good a breakfast in all his life.

When Toad had taken as much stew on board as he thought he could possibly hold, he got up and took an affectionate farewell of the horse; and the gypsy, who knew the riverside well, gave him directions which way to go, and he set forth on his travels again in the best possible spirits. The sun was shining brightly, his wet clothes were quite dry, he had money in his pockets once more, and he had had a substantial meal, hot and nourishing, and felt big, and strong, and self-confident.

As he tramped along gaily, he thought of his adventures and escapes, and how when things seemed at their worst he had always managed to find a way out; and his pride and conceit began to swell within him. He got so puffed up that he made up a song in praise of himself, and sang it at the top of his voice. It was perhaps the most conceited song that any animal ever composed:

> *The world has held great Heroes,*
> *As history-books have showed;*
> *But never a name to go down to fame*
> *Compared with that of Toad!*
>
> *The clever men at Oxford*
> *Know all that there is to be knowed.*
> *But they none of them know one half as much*
> *As intelligent Mr Toad!*
>
> *The Queen and her Ladies-in-waiting*
> *Sat at the window and sewed.*
> *She cried, "Look! who's that* handsome *man?"*
> *They answered, "Mr Toad."*

There was a great deal more, but too dreadfully conceited to be written down. These are some of the milder verses.

He sang as he walked, and walked as he sang. But his pride was shortly to have a severe fall.

After some miles he reached the high road, and as he turned into it and glanced along its white length, he saw approaching him a speck that turned into a dot and then a blob, and then into something very familiar; and a "poop, poop!" fell on his delighted ear.

"This is something like!" said the excited Toad. "This is real life again, this is the world from which I have been missed so long! I will hail them, my brothers of the wheel, and they will give me a lift, and, with luck, it may even end in my driving up to Toad Hall! That will be one in the eye for Badger!"

He stepped out into the road to hail the motor-car, which came along at an easy pace, when suddenly he became very pale, his knees shook, and he doubled up with a sickening pain in his interior. And well he might, for the approaching car was the very one he had stolen out of the yard of the Red Lion Hotel! And the people in it were the very same people he had sat and watched at luncheon in the coffee-room! He sank down in a heap, murmuring, "It's all up! Prison again! Dry bread and water!"

The motor-car drew nearer till at last he heard it stop. Two gentlemen got out and one of them said, "O dear! this is very sad! A poor washerwoman has fainted in the road! Perhaps she is overcome by the heat, poor creature. Let us lift her into the car and take her to the nearest village, where doubtless she has friends."

They tenderly lifted Toad into the motor-car and propped him up with soft cushions, and proceeded on their way.

When Toad knew that he was not recognized, his courage began to revive, and he opened first one eye, then the other.

"Look!" said one of the gentlemen, "she is better already. The fresh air is doing her good. How do you feel now, ma'am?"

"Thank you kindly, sir," said Toad in a feeble voice, "I'm feeling a great deal better! I was thinking, if I might sit on the front seat there, beside the driver, where I could get the fresh air full in my face, I should soon be all right again."

"What a sensible woman!" said the gentleman. "Of course you shall." So they helped Toad into the front seat beside the driver, and on they went once more.

Toad was almost himself again by now. And he turned to the driver at his side. "Please, sir," he said, "I wish you would let me try and drive a little. It looks so easy and I should like to be able to tell my friends that once I had driven a motor-car!"

The driver laughed so heartily that the gentleman inquired what the matter was. When he heard, he said, "Bravo, ma'am! I like your spirit. Let her have a try."

Toad scrambled into the driver's seat, took the steering-wheel in his hands, listened to the instructions given him, and set the car in motion, very slowly and carefully.

The gentlemen behind clapped their hands and applauded, saying, "How well she does it! Fancy a washerwoman driving a car as well as that, the first time!"

Toad went a little faster; then faster still, and faster.

He heard the gentlemen call out, "Be careful, washerwoman!" And this annoyed him, and he began to lose his head.

The driver tried to interfere, but he pinned him down with one elbow, and put on full speed. "Washerwoman, indeed!" he shouted recklessly. "Ho, ho! I am the Toad, the motor-car snatcher, the prison-breaker, the Toad who always escapes!"

With a cry of horror the party flung themselves on him. "Seize him!" they cried. "Seize the Toad who stole our motor-car!"

Alas! they should have remembered to stop the motor-car before playing pranks of that sort. With a half-turn of the wheel Toad sent the car crashing through the low roadside hedge. One mighty bound, a violent shock, and the wheels of the car were churning up the thick mud of a horse-pond.

Toad found himself flying through the air with the delicate curve of a swallow. He liked the motion, and was just beginning to wonder whether he would develop wings when he landed with a thump, in the soft rich grass of a meadow. Sitting up, he could just see the car in the pond; the gentlemen and driver were floundering helplessly in the water. He picked himself up and set off running across country as hard as he could, till he was breathless and weary, and had to settle into an easy walk. When he had recovered his breath and was able to think calmly, he began to laugh, and he laughed till he had to sit down under a hedge. "Ho, ho!" he cried. "Toad, as usual, comes out on top! Who got them to give him a lift? Who persuaded them into letting him drive? Who landed them all in a horse-pond? Who escaped, flying gaily through the air, leaving them in the mud? Why, Toad, of course; clever Toad, great Toad, *good* Toad! How clever I am! How clever, how very clev—"

A slight noise behind him made him turn his head and look. O horror!

About two fields off, a chauffeur in his leather gaiters and two large rural policemen were running towards him as hard as they could go!

Toad pelted away again. "O my!" he gasped. "O my! O my!"

He glanced back, and saw to his dismay that they were gaining on him. On he ran. He did his best, but he was a fat animal, and his legs were short, and still they gained. He could hear them close behind him now. He struggled on wildly, looking back over his shoulder at the enemy, when suddenly the earth failed under his feet, he grasped at the air, and—

splash! he found himself head over ears in deep, rapid water;

in his panic he had run straight into the river!

He rose to the surface and tried to grasp the reeds and rushes that grew along the water's edge, but the stream was so strong it tore them out of his hands. "O my!" gasped Toad, "if ever I steal a motor-car again!" Then down he went, and came up breathless and spluttering. Presently he saw a big dark hole in the bank, just above his head, and as the stream bore him past, he reached up and caught hold of the edge and held on. Slowly and with difficulty he drew himself up out of the water. There he remained for some minutes, puffing and panting.

As he stared before him into the dark hole, some bright small thing shone and twinkled in its depths, moving towards him.

A face grew up around it, a familiar face!

Brown and small, with whiskers.

Grave and round, with neat ears and silky hair.

It was the Water Rat!

FOUR

The Return of Toad

The Rat put out a paw, gripped Toad by the scruff of the neck, and gave a great hoist and pull; and the waterlogged Toad came up over the edge of the hole till at last he stood in the hall, streaked with mud and weed, but happy and high-spirited, now that he found himself once more in the house of a friend.

"O Ratty!" he cried. "I've been through such times since I saw you last, you can't think! Just hold on till I tell you—"

"Toad," said the Water Rat, "go upstairs at once, and take off that old cotton rag that looks as if it belonged to some washer-woman. I'll have something to say to you later!"

Toad was at first inclined to stop and do some talking back at him. He had had enough of being ordered about in prison. However, he caught sight of himself in the looking-glass over the hatstand, with the rusty black bonnet perched rakishly over one eye, and he changed his mind and went very quickly upstairs to the Rat's dressing-room.

By the time he came down again luncheon was on the table. While they ate, Toad told the Rat all his adventures. The more he talked, the more grave and silent the Rat became.

When at last Toad had talked himself to a standstill, the Rat said, "Now, Toady, seriously, don't you see what a fool you've been making of yourself? You've been handcuffed, imprisoned, starved, chased, insulted and ignominiously flung into the water. Where's the amusement in that? Where does the fun come in? And all because you must needs go and steal a motor-car. You've never had anything but trouble from the moment you set eyes on one. Think of your friends. Do you suppose it's any pleasure to me to hear animals saying I'm the chap that keeps company with jail-birds?"

Toad heaved a deep sigh and said, "Quite right, Ratty! I've been a conceited fool, I can see that. As for motor-cars, I've not been so keen about them since my last ducking in that river of yours. The fact is, I've had enough of adventures. I shall lead a quiet life, pottering about Toad Hall; and I shall keep a pony-chaise to jog about the country in, as I used to in the old days."

"Do you mean you haven't *heard*?" cried the Rat.

"Heard what?" said Toad, turning pale.

"About the Stoats and Weasels?"

"No!" cried Toad. "What have they been doing?"

"They've been and taken Toad Hall!"

A large tear welled up in each of Toad's eyes, overflowed and splashed on the table, plop! plop!

"When you got into that—trouble of yours," said the Rat, "it was a good deal talked about down here. Animals took sides. The River-bankers stuck up for you. But the Wild Wood animals said hard things, served you right. You were done for this time! You would never come back again, never! And one night, a band of weasels and ferrets and stoats broke into Toad Hall, and have been living there ever since!"

"O, have they!" said Toad, getting up and seizing a stick. "I'll jolly soon see about that!"

"It's no good!" called the Rat after him. "You'll only get into trouble."

But there was no holding the Toad. He marched down the road, his stick over his shoulder, till he got near his front gate, when suddenly there popped up from behind the palings a long yellow ferret with a gun.

"Who comes there?" said the ferret sharply.

"What do you mean by talking like that to me?" said Toad very angrily. "Come out or I'll—"

The ferret said never a word, but brought his gun to his shoulder. Toad dropped flat in the road and *Bang!* a bullet whistled over his head.

The startled Toad scrambled to his feet and scampered down the road; and as he ran he heard the ferret laughing a horrid, thin little laugh.

He went back, got out the boat, and set off rowing up river to where the garden of Toad Hall came down to the waterside.

Arriving within sight of his old home, he rested on his oars

and surveyed the land cautiously.

All seemed very peaceful and deserted. He would try the boat-house first, he thought. Very warily he paddled up the creek, and was just passing under the bridge, when . . . *Crash!*

A great stone, dropped from above, smashed through the bottom of the boat. It filled and sank, and Toad found himself struggling in deep water. Looking up, he saw two stoats leaning over the parapet of the bridge, watching him with glee. "It will be your head next time, Toady!" they called out to him. Toad swam to shore while the stoats laughed and laughed.

"Well, *what* did I tell you?" said the Rat crossly, when Toad related his disappointing experiences. "And now you've been and lost me my boat! And simply ruined that nice suit I lent you! Really, Toad, be patient. We can do nothing until we have seen the Mole and the Badger."

"O, ah, yes, the Mole and the Badger," said Toad. "What's become of the dear fellows? I had forgotten all about them."

"Well may you ask!" said the Rat reproachfully. "While you were riding about in motor-cars, and breakfasting on the fat of the land, those two animals have been camping out in every sort of weather, watching over your house, contriving how to get it back for you. You don't deserve such loyal friends, Toad, you don't, really."

"I know," sobbed Toad. "Let me go and find them, and share their hardships, and—Hold on! Supper's here, hooray!"

They had just finished their meal when there came a heavy knock at the door, and in walked Mr Badger. His shoes were covered with mud, and he was looking rough and tousled; but then he had never been very smart, Badger. He came solemnly up to Toad, shook him by the paw, and said, "Welcome home, Toad!" Then he helped himself to a large slice of cold pie.

Presently there came another, lighter knock and the Rat ushered in the Mole, very shabby and unwashed, with bits of hay and straw sticking in his fur.

The Adventures of Mr Toad

"Toad!" cried the Mole, beaming. "Fancy having you back! We never dreamt you would turn up so soon! Why, you must have managed to escape, you clever Toad!"

The Rat pulled him by the elbow; but it was too late.

"Clever? O no!" said Toad. "Not according to my friends. I've only broken out of the strongest prison in England, that's all! And captured a railway train and escaped on it, that's all! And disguised myself and gone about the country humbugging everybody, that's all! O no! I'm a stupid fool, I am!"

He straddled the hearth-rug, thrust his paw into his pocket and pulled out a handful of silver. "Look at that!" he cried, displaying it. "Not bad for a few minutes' work! And how do you think I done it, Mole? Horse-dealing! That's how!"

"Toad, be quiet!" said the Rat. "And don't you egg him on, Mole, when you know what he is; tell us what the position is, now Toad is back at last."

"About as bad as it can be," replied the Mole. "Badger and I have been round and round the place; always the same thing. Sentries posted everywhere, guns poked out at us, always an animal on the look-out, and when they see us, my! how they laugh! That's what annoys me most!"

The Badger, having finished his pie, got up from his seat and stood before the fireplace.

"Toad!" he said severely. "You bad little animal! Aren't you ashamed of yourself? Think what your father would have said if he had been here tonight, and known of all your goings-on! What Mole says is true. The stoats are on guard, at every point. It's quite useless to think of attacking the place."

"Then it's all over," sobbed the Toad. "I shall go and enlist for a soldier, and never see my dear Toad Hall any more!"

"Cheer up, Toady!" said the Badger. "There are more ways of getting back a place than taking it by storm. I haven't said my last word yet. Now I'm going to tell you a secret."

Toad dried his eyes. Secrets had an immense attraction for him, because he never could keep one.

"There—is—an—underground—passage," said the Badger impressively, "that leads from the river bank quite near here, right up into the middle of Toad Hall."

"Nonsense! Badger," said Toad airily. "You've been listening to some of the yarns they spin in the public-houses about here. I know every inch of Toad Hall, inside and out. Nothing of the sort, I do assure you!"

"My young friend," said the Badger with severity, "your father, who was a worthy animal—a lot worthier than some I know—was a particular friend of mine, and told me a great deal he wouldn't have dreamt of telling you. He discovered that passage—of course it was made hundreds of years before he ever came to live there—and he repaired it and cleaned it out, because he thought it might come in useful some day, in case of trouble or danger, and he showed it to me. 'Don't let my son know about it,' he said. 'He's a good boy, but simply cannot hold his tongue. If he's ever in a real fix, and it would be of use to him, you may tell him about the secret passage; but not before.'"

The other animals looked to see how Toad would take it.

"Well," he said, "perhaps I am a bit of a talker. A popular fellow such as I am—my friends get round me—and somehow my tongue gets wagging. I have the gift of conversation. I've been told I ought to have a *salon*, whatever that may be. Go on, Badger. How's this passage of yours going to help us?"

"I've found out a thing or two lately," continued the Badger. "There's going to be a big banquet tomorrow night. It's somebody's birthday—the Chief Weasel's, I believe—and all the weasels will be gathered in the dining-hall, eating and drinking and carrying on, suspecting nothing. No guns, no swords, no sticks, no arms of any sort whatever!"

"But the sentinels will be posted as usual," remarked the Rat.

"Exactly," said the Badger; "that is my point. The weasels will trust entirely to their sentinels. That is where the passage comes in. That useful tunnel leads right up under the butler's pantry, next to the dining-hall!"

"Aha! that squeaky board in the butler's pantry!" said Toad. "Now I understand it!"

"We shall creep out into the pantry—" cried the Mole.

"—with our pistols, swords and sticks—" shouted the Rat.

"—and rush in upon them," said the Badger.

"—and whack 'em,"

"and whack 'em,"

"and whack 'em!" cried the Toad in ecstasy, running round and round the room.

"Very well, then," said the Badger, "our plan is settled and there's nothing more to argue about. So, as it's getting late, all of you go off to bed at once. We will make the necessary arrangements in the morning."

Toad slept late next morning, and by the time he got down, found the other animals had finished their breakfast some time before. The Mole had slipped off by himself, without telling anyone where he was going. The Badger sat in the armchair, reading the paper, and the Rat was running round the room busily, distributing weapons in four little heaps on the floor.

Presently the Mole came tumbling into the room, evidently pleased with himself. "I've been having such fun!" he began; "I've been getting a rise out of the stoats!"

"I hope you've been careful, Mole?" said the Rat.

"I hope so, too," said the Mole. "I got the idea when I found Toad's old washerwoman-dress hanging in the kitchen. I put it on, and off I went to Toad Hall, as bold as you please. 'Good morning, gentlemen!' says I. 'Want any washing done today?'

"They looked at me very proud and stiff and haughty, and said, 'Go away, washerwoman! We don't do washing on duty.' 'Or any other time?' says I. Ho, ho, ho! Some of the stoats turned quite pink, and the sergeant said, 'Run away, my good woman!' 'Run away?' says I; 'it won't be me running away, in a very short time from now!'"

"O, *Moly,* how could you?" said the Rat, dismayed.

The Badger laid down his paper.

"I could see them pricking up their ears and looking at each other," went on the Mole; "and the sergeant said to them, 'Never mind *her;* she doesn't know what she's talking about.'

"'O! don't I?' said I. 'Well, my daughter washes for Mr Badger, and that'll show you whether I know! A hundred bloodthirsty Badgers are going to attack Toad Hall this very night, by way of the paddock. Six boat-loads of rats will come up the river while a picked body of toads, known as the Die-hards, or the Death-or-Glory Toads, will storm the orchard and carry everything before them. There won't be much left of you to wash, by the time they've done with you.' Then I ran away and hid;

and presently I came creeping back along the ditch and took a peep at them through the hedge. They were all as nervous as could be, running all ways at once, and I heard them saying 'That's *just* like the weasels; they're to stop comfortably in the banqueting-hall, and have feasting and songs and all sorts of fun, while we must stay on guard in the cold and dark, and be cut to pieces by bloodthirsty Badgers!'"

"You silly fool, Mole!" cried Toad. "You've been and spoilt everything!"

"Mole," said the Badger. "You have managed excellently. I begin to have great hopes of you. Clever Mole!"

The Toad was wild with jealousy, especially as he couldn't make out for the life of him what the Mole had done that was so clever; fortunately for him, before he could show temper, the bell rang for luncheon.

It was a simple but sustaining meal—bacon and broad beans, and a macaroni pudding; and when they had done, the Badger settled himself into an arm-chair, and said, "I'm just going to take forty winks, while I can." And he was soon snoring. The anxious Rat resumed his preparations, running between his heaps. So the Mole drew his arm through Toad's, led him into the open air, shoved him into a wicker chair, and made him tell all his adventures from beginning to end. Toad rather let himself go. Indeed, much he related belonged more to the category of what-might-have-happened-had-I-only-thought-of-it-in-time-instead-of-ten-minutes-afterwards. Those are always the best and the raciest adventures; and why should they not be ours, as much as the things that really come off?

When it began to grow dark, the Rat summoned them back into the parlour, stood each of them alongside his little heap, and proceeded to dress them up for the coming expedition. First, there was a belt to go round each animal, then a sword to be stuck into each belt, and then a cutlass on the other side to balance it. Then a pair of pistols, a policeman's truncheon, several sets of handcuffs, some bandages and sticking-plaster, and a flask and a sandwich-case. The Badger laughed and said, "I'm going to do all I've got to do with this here stick." But the Rat only said, "*Please,* Badger! You know I shouldn't like you to say I had forgotten *anything!*"

When all was quite ready, the Badger took a lantern in one paw, grasped his great stick with the other, and said, "Now then, follow me!"

The Badger led the animals along by the river for a little way, and then into a hole in the bank. At last they were in the secret passage, and the expedition had begun! It was low and narrow, and Toad began to shiver from dread of what might be before him. The lantern was far ahead, and he could not help lagging behind in the darkness. He heard the Rat call out "*Come* on, Toad!" and a terror seized him of being left alone, and he "came on" with such a rush that he upset the Rat into the Mole and the Mole into the Badger, and all was confusion. They groped and shuffled along, with their ears pricked up and their paws on their pistols, till at last the Badger said, "We ought to be nearly under the Hall."

Then suddenly they heard, far away as it might be, and yet nearly over their heads, shouting and cheering and stamping on the floor. Toad's terrors all returned, but the Badger only remarked, "They *are* going it, the weasels!"

The passage now began to slope upwards; and the noise broke out again, quite distinct this time, and very close above them. "Ooo-ray-oo-ray-oo-ray-ooray!" they heard, and the stamping of feet on the floor, and clinking of glasses as fists pounded on the table. "Come on!" said Badger. They hurried along till the passage came to a full stop, and they found themselves standing under the trap-door that led up into the butler's pantry.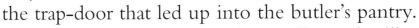

The Badger said, "Now, boys, all together!" and the four of them heaved the trap-door back.

The noise, as they emerged, was simply deafening. As the cheering and hammering slowly subsided, a voice could be made out saying, "Before I resume my seat I should like to say one word about our kind host, Mr Toad. We all know Toad! *Good* Toad, *modest* Toad, *honest* Toad!"

"Let me get at him!" muttered Toad, grinding his teeth.

"Hold hard a minute!" said the Badger, restraining him with difficulty. "Get ready, all of you!"

"Let me sing you a song," went on the voice, "which I have composed on the subject of Toad—" Then the Chief Weasel—for it was he—began in a high, squeaky voice:

> *Toad he went a-pleasuring*
> *Gaily down the street—*

The Badger drew himself up, took a firm grip of his stick, and cried: "Follow me!" And flung the door open.

83

My! What a squealing and squeaking filled the air!
Well might the weasels spring at the windows!
Well might the ferrets rush for the chimney!
Well might tables and chairs be upset,
and glass and china be sent crashing
on the floor, in the panic of that
terrible moment when the four
Heroes strode into the room!
The mighty Badger, his whiskers
bristling, his great cudgel whistling
through the air; Mole, black and grim,
brandishing his stick, shouting his
awful war-cry, "A Mole! A Mole!"
Rat, desperate and determined, his
belt bulging with weapons of every
age and variety; Toad, swollen to
twice his ordinary size, emitting
Toad-whoops that chilled them
to the marrow! "Toad he went
a-pleasuring!" he yelled.
"I'll pleasure 'em!" and
he went straight for
the Chief Weasel.

Up and down strode the four Friends, whacking every head that showed itself; and in five minutes the room was cleared. Through the broken windows the shrieks of escaping weasels were borne faintly to their ears; on the floor lay some dozen or so of the enemy, on whom the Mole was busily engaged in fitting handcuffs. The Badger wiped his brow.

"Mole," he said, "you're the best of fellows! Just cut along outside, and see what those sentries are doing. I've an idea that, thanks to you, we shan't have much trouble from *them!*"

Then he said in that rather common way he had of speaking, "Stir your stumps, Toad! We've got your house back for you, and you don't offer us so much as a sandwich."

Toad felt hurt that the Badger didn't say pleasant things to him, as he had to the Mole, and tell him what a fine fellow he was, and how splendidly he had fought; for he was rather pleased with himself and the way he had sent the Chief Weasel flying across the table. But he bustled about, and so did the Rat, and soon they found some guava jelly in a glass dish, and a cold chicken, some trifle, and quite a lot of lobster salad; and in the pantry they came upon a basket of French rolls and any quantity of cheese, butter, and celery. They were just about to sit down when the Mole clambered in through the window, chuckling, with an armful of rifles.

"It's all over," he reported. "From what I can make out, as soon as the stoats, who were very nervous and jumpy already, heard the shrieks inside the hall, they threw down their rifles and fled. So *that's* all right!"

Then Toad, like the gentleman he was, put all jealousy from him and said, "Thank you, Mole, for your trouble tonight and especially for your cleverness this morning!" So they finished their supper in great joy and contentment, safe in Toad's ancestral home; won back by matchless valour, consummate strategy, and a proper handling of sticks.

After this climax, the four animals continued to lead their lives, undisturbed by further invasions.

Sometimes, in the long summer evenings, the friends would take a stroll together in the Wild Wood, now tamed so far as they were concerned; and it was pleasing to see how respectfully they were greeted by the inhabitants; mother-weasels would bring their young ones to the mouths of their holes, and say, pointing, "Look! There goes the great Mr Toad! And that's the Water Rat, a terrible fighter. And yonder comes the famous Mr Mole, of whom you've heard your father tell!" But when their infants were fractious and quite beyond control, they would quiet them by telling how, if they didn't hush, the terrible grey Badger would up and get them. This was a base libel on Badger, who, though he cared little about Society, was rather fond of children; but it never failed to have its full effect.